Earl's Too Cool for Me

Earl's Too Cool for Me

by Leah Komaiko
illustrated by Laura Cornell

Laura Geringer Books
An Imprint of HarperCollinsPublishers

Library of Congress Cataloging-in-Publication Data
Komaiko, Leah.
    Earl's too cool for me / Leah Komaiko ; illustrated
by Laura Cornell.
        p.   cm.
    Summary: The antics and adventures of cool boy
Earl include riding on the Milky Way, growing a rose
from his fingernails, and swinging with gorillas.
    ISBN 0-06-051914-2 (pbk.)
[1. Stories in rhyme.] I. Cornell, Laura, ill. II. Title.
PZ8.3.K835 Ear 1988   87-30803
[E]—dc19   CIP
                                              AC

Visit us on the World Wide Web!
www.harperchildrens.com

Earl's got a bicycle made of hay.

He takes rides on the Milky Way.

Earl's too cool for me.

Earl's got a hat with a real horse feather.
He wears socks made of chicken leather.

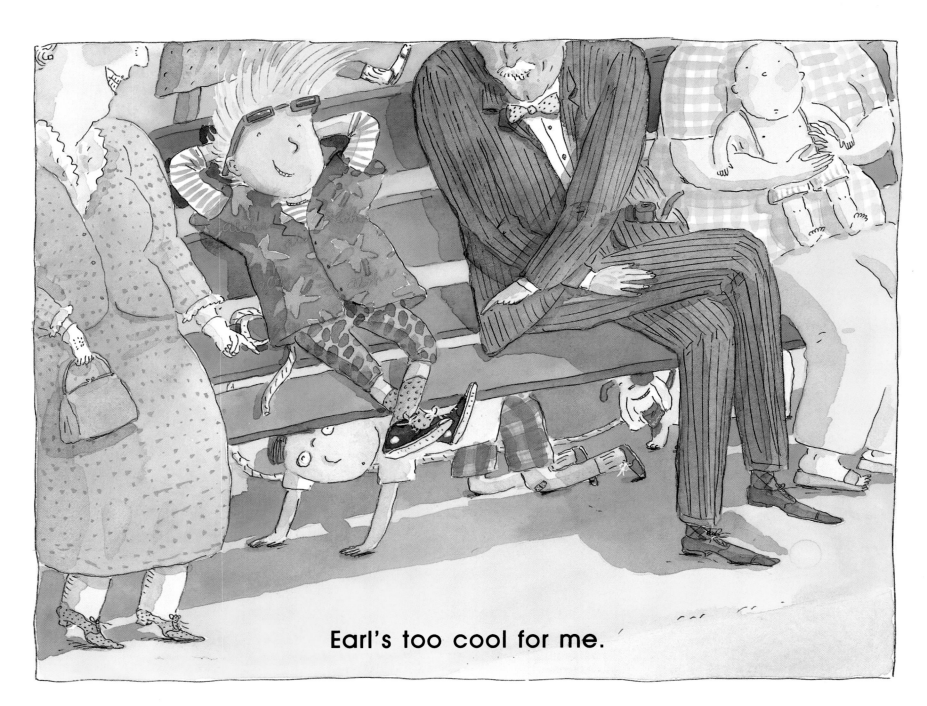

Earl's too cool for me.

Earl knows all the letters in the Zulu alphabet.
He caught wild boars in a butterfly net.

Earl's too cool for me.

Earl's been to France and South Zanzibar.
He drove to China in an egg roll car.

Earl's too cool for me.

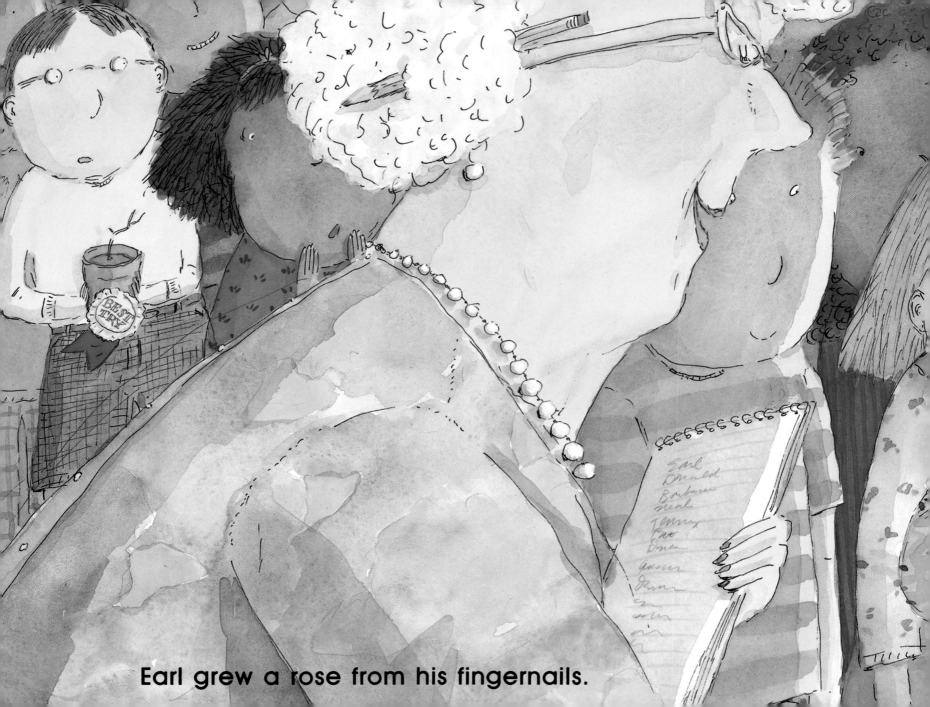

Earl grew a rose from his fingernails.

He once turned green for the Prince of Wales.

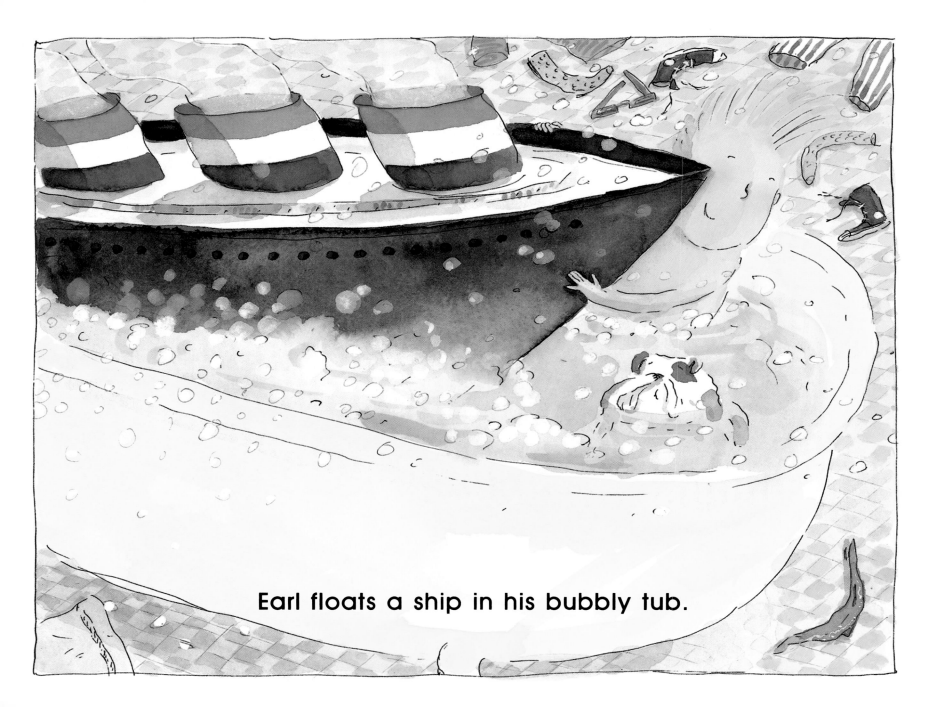

Earl floats a ship in his bubbly tub.

He taught an octopus how to scrub.

Earl's too cool for me.

Earl swings with gorillas—and when he's tired of that—

He plays jazz with the alley cat.

Earl's too cool for me.

Earl's friendly with the Martians and a few movie stars.

He keeps monster eyes in empty jelly jars.

Earl's too cool for me.

Now here comes Earl,

I'm not cool like he is—

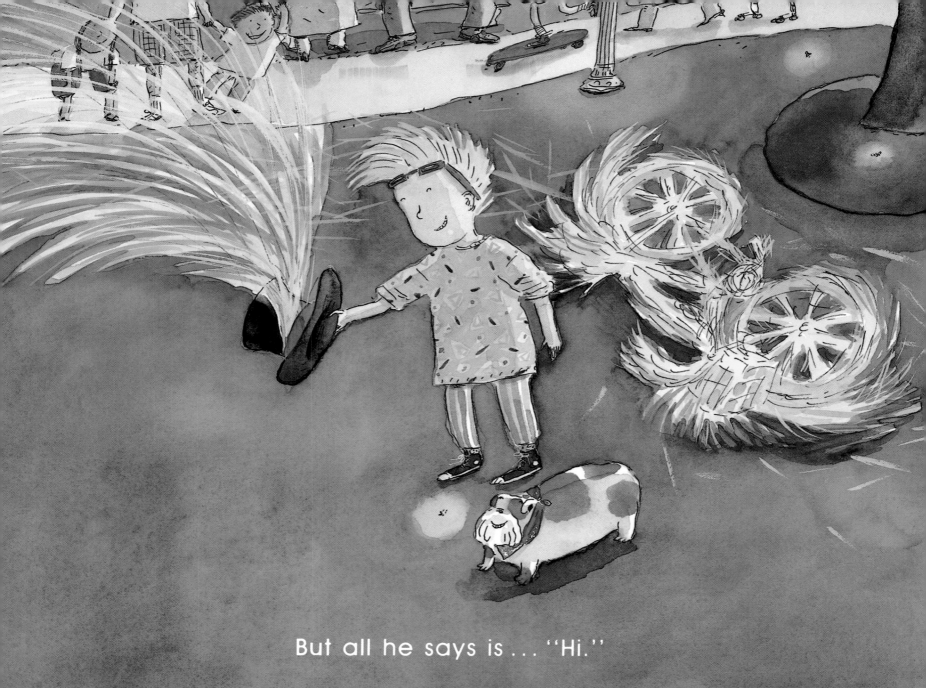

But all he says is ... "Hi."

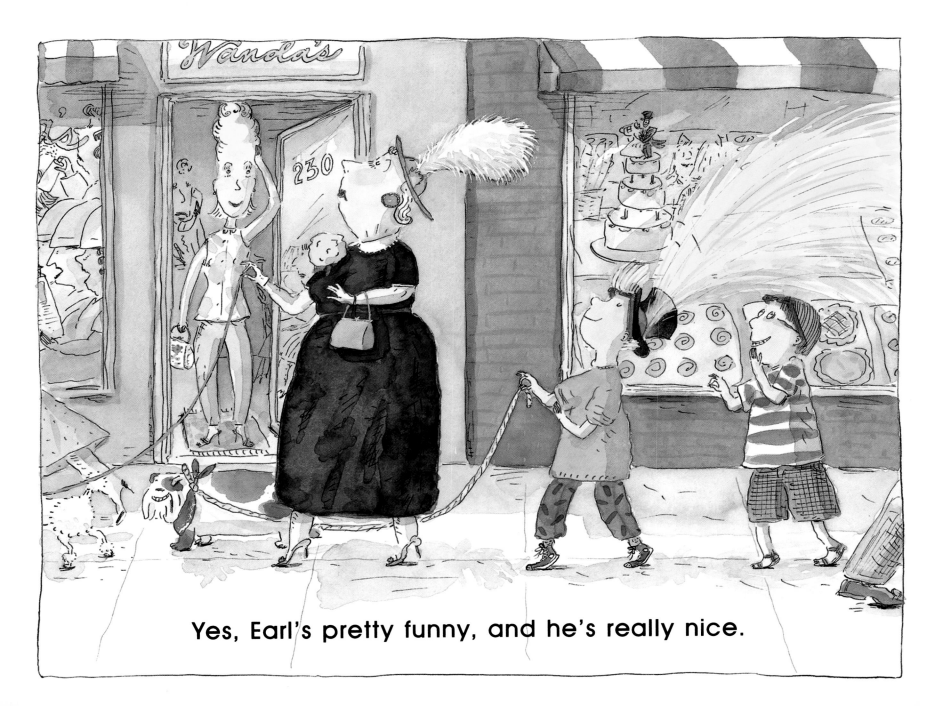

Yes, Earl's pretty funny, and he's really nice.

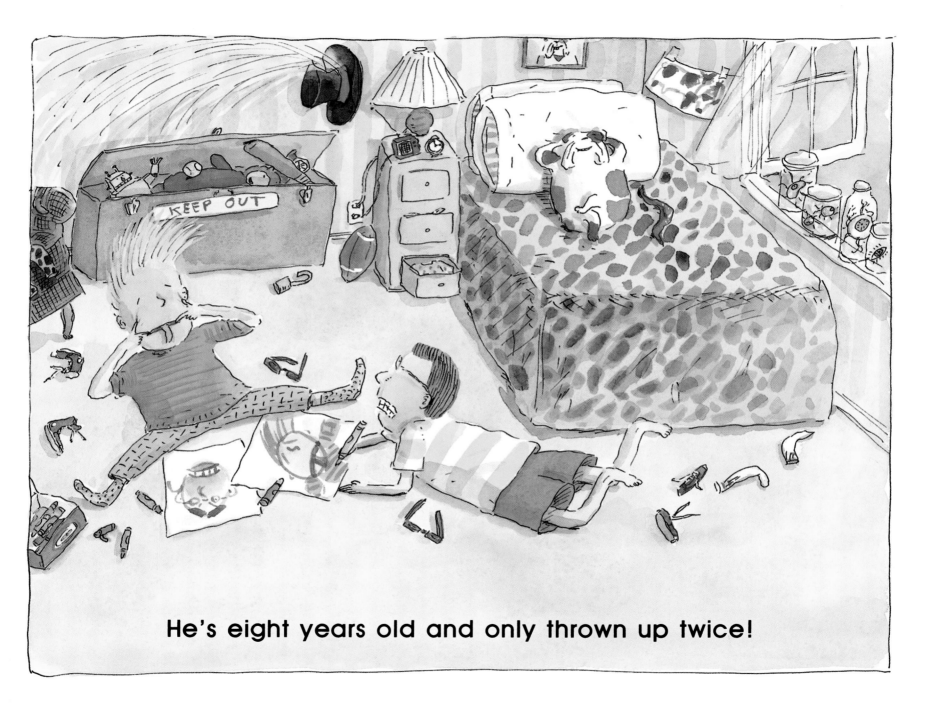

He's eight years old and only thrown up twice!

We're cool as cool can be.